Nelly Buchet is the author of a dozen books for young readers, including ALA Notable *Cat Dog Dog: The Story of a Blended Family* (Random House Studio, with art by Andrea Zuill), which was chosen by children around the world as the 2021 Irma Black Award for Excellence in Children's Literature winner. She has taught nonviolent conflict resolution in schools and created a nonprofit project that brings picture books to refugee children through orphanages and libraries. French American, Nelly lives in Berlin and loves dance and dogs, preferably together.

You can find her online at her website nellybuchet.com,
or on Instagram @nellybuchetbooks.

Rachel Katstaller is an illustrator from tiny tropical El Salvador. After attending the Summer Residency in Illustration at the School of Visual Arts in New York City in 2014, Rachel decided to pursue her lifelong dream of becoming a children's book illustrator. Since then, Rachel has relocated to the Austrian Alps along with her cat, Hemingway.

You can find her at her website rachelkatstaller.com,
or on Instagram @rachelkatstaller.

For my little sister with the long coat — N. B.
To my chosen sisters Estefanía, Laura, and Paola — R. K.

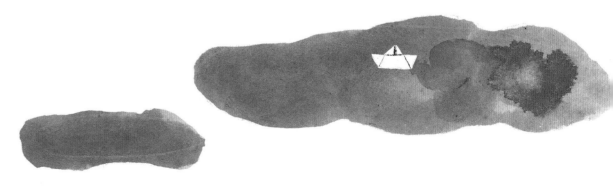

Written by Nelly Buchet

Illustrated by Rachel Katstaller

North
South

We were supposed to have the best day.

But it was really hot,

like, superhot—

legs-stick-to-the-seat hot.

And way too crowded! There were people everywhere.

I was so thirsty!

Then it started raining.

More like pouring.

We had to change our plans.

We had to change our new plans too!

There were lines everywhere.

The library was closing.

We were soaked.

And hungry.

With nowhere to go.

So we went home.

The day wasn't what I expected.

Like, at all.

It was better.

I think.

I mean, how bad can it be—

when my big sister's with me?

I have two sisters: a big one and a little one.
So I'm both a little sister and a big one.
Rachel, the illustrator of this book,
doesn't have sisters. She has brothers!
What about you? Do you have siblings?
Do you have a friend you love so much
that they feel like a sibling?

My sisters and I have a lot of fun together.
But sometimes, like in this book, things
just don't go as planned. It can feel like the
worst day ever! We've all had bad days. . . .
And it can be for the better. You never
know how a day can turn around. Life is
full of surprises!
Can you think of a time when you had to
change your plans? What was something
fun you did instead?

—Nelly Buchet